Bear Can Dance!

Suzanne Bloom

BOYDS MILLS PRESS

AN IMPRINT OF HIGHLIGHTS

Honesdale, Pennsylvania

Boyds Mills Press
An Imprint of Highlights
815 Church Street
Honesdale, Pennsylvania 18431
boydsmillspress.com
Printed in China
ISBN 978-1-62979-442-6
Library of Congress Control Number: 2014958543

First edition
10 9 8 7 6 5 4 3 2 1

Production by Sue Cole
The text of this book is set in ITC Legacy Sans.
The illustrations are done in pastel.

Para mi amiga Xelena, que tiene un corazón bailando.
(For my friend Xelena, who has a dancing heart.)

I wish I could fly.

Why, Bear?

So I could swoop and glide
and feel the wind in my fur.

Oh, Bear,
    I wish I could help.

I'll show you.
I'll show you how to fly.
It's easy breezy.

First, you need the proper equipment.

Now flap, flap, flap,
and whoosh around.

I don't feel whooshy.
I feel woozy.

Wait. I have a better idea.

Do you feel swoopy?
Do you feel the wind in your fur?

No. I feel wobbly.
This is not working.
I cannot fly!

Wait.
I have a better better idea.

No, no.
Bear cannot fly.

But look, Goosey.
Bear is swooping and gliding.

Bear is dancing.

Bear can dance?

It's like flying, but with your
feet on the ground. Mostly.

Ohhhh.
Bear can dance!

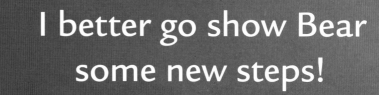

I better go show Bear
some new steps!